# My Island Grandma

Kathryn Lasky

Illustrated by

Amy Schwartz

Morrow Junior Books  New York

*For Rusty,*
*the original Island Grandma*
—K.L.

Watercolors and colored pencils were used for the full-color artwork. The text type is 15-point Goudy Oldstyle.

Text copyright © 1979, 1993 by Kathryn Lasky. Illustrations copyright © 1993 by Amy Schwartz

Printed in Hong Kong by South China Printing Company (1988) Ltd.
1  2  3  4  5  6  7  8  9  10

Library of Congress Cataloging-in-Publication Data
Lasky, Kathryn. My island grandma/by Kathryn Lasky; illustrated by Amy Schwartz. p.   cm.
Summary: Abbey spends every summer with her parents and her grandmother on an island, where the leisurely activities include swimming in the ocean, picking blueberries, and finding the constellations.
ISBN 0-688-07946-6 (trade.)—ISBN 0-688-07948-2 (lib.)
[1. Islands—Fiction.  2. Grandmothers—Fiction.  3. Summer—Fiction.]  I. Schwartz, Amy, ill.  II. Title.
PZ7.L3274My  1993 [E]—dc20    91-31000    CIP    AC

I have a grandmother who swims in dark sea pools. She takes me with her early in the morning.

She has strong hands that hold me tight and safe in the cool, deep water while I learn to swim.

Today she held me with two hands and I kicked my feet. Tomorrow when she holds me with one hand, I will almost float.

And the next day she will hold me with just her finger and I *will* float.

The day after that no hands, no fingers, and I will swim away!

Grandma's hands are strong from taking down the big shutters every June from her cabin windows, and from digging the summer garden, pumping buckets full of cold water at the well, and carrying logs for the wood-burning stove.

It's very different on an island and we live there all summer long.

In June, after my dad closes up his classroom and my mom packs her paint box full of summer colors, we drive away from the city. We drive all through the night and day until we come to the ocean, where we leave our car behind and ride on a ferryboat to the island.

Grandma and her dog, Shadow, are already there, waiting with a wheelbarrow to carry our suitcases to our cabin.

There is a secret path through the woods between our cabin and hers. The ground is green and soft with moss that feels like a velvet blanket underneath my feet. The sunlight twinkles through the giant pine trees. It's a greenlight world and Grandma's cabin is on the other side by the sea.

I visit her whenever I want. I just run barefoot down the green moss path, to the edge of the forest where she lives. Every day Grandma and I do wonderful summer things.

After swimming in the morning we sit on a million-year-old rock and wrap ourselves up in big towels and we talk about things.

On our way home Grandma picks sea herbs that grow along the shore to make salad. Sometimes she gathers periwinkles, little sea snails that live on rocks, to make soup.

I hate them both.

But I love to eat the blueberries we pick in the afternoon. When we pick the berries I pretend that I am a little bear, just like the one in the story Grandma read to me, and that she is the mother bear. I growl and do bear things. I snap at her with my lips pulled over my teeth so it won't hurt. That's how baby bears get their mother's attention.

One time on our way back from picking blueberries, Grandma called to me very softly, "Come over here, Abbey, and look at this."

I knew from her whispery voice that I should walk very quietly. So I tiptoed, and when I got to where Grandma was kneeling, I saw a nest of dried grass at her feet. In the nest were three eggs—brown and gray with little speckles all over them.

One egg was jiggling just as if excited little feelings were all closed up inside.

Then the egg bumped and rolled over, showing a big, bloody gash.

"Did it hurt itself?" I asked.

"No," Grandma said, "that's the blood that comes with new life."

Inside the bloody gash I could see a small beak, tinier than my little fingernail, pecking its way out of the egg.

Grandma said we had to go and pointed to the mother duck flying above. "She's angry that we're even near."

"But I want to stay! I really want to see this baby duck get born!"

"Absolutely not, Abbey. When you're getting born, you need to be left with your own kind. People with people, ducks with ducks."

But I wanted to stay so badly. I really did.

Sometimes we go sailing, Grandma and Shadow and me. We sail in a little boat called *Memory*. It's painted white with a bright green stripe, and Grandma's the skipper. She steers with the tiller and I hold the ropes for the sail and pull them at important times.

When we are sailing in *Memory* and there are lots of big clouds in the sky, we tell cloud stories.

We look up in the sky and find special shapes in the clouds.

Once I said, "Look, Grandma! Remember the shark Daddy told us about? There it is swimming in the sky chasing the baby seal. It won't catch it this time because there's a cloud cave—see it? And it's just big enough for the seal pup to hide in."

Grandma says my stories are scary. She tells cloud stories about lambs and camels and sometimes disobedient children who don't eat their vegetables. And I always say, "Please, Grandma, no vegetable stories allowed. Just stories about plain bad children."

We make things on rainy days. We make moss gardens in old pie tins. We fill the pie tin with dirt and cover the dirt with thick green moss. Then we stick in the smallest plants. And if you look at the moss garden for a while, it becomes a tiny world with little green mountains and little trees and valleys.

Sometimes we make moon cookies and star cookies and put silver sprinkles on them.

Grandma made me a special sleeping bag for when I spend the night. The lining is dark blue with pink and lavender flowers. Inside it feels just like sleeping in a flower cave with flowers growing everywhere—out of the ceiling, out of the walls, out of the floor.

I love to shine my flashlight in the flower cave in the middle of the night. I crawl way down to the foot of the bag where it is so dark you can breathe the blackness, and then I press the flashlight button and suddenly there are a million flowers jumping and hopping all over.

And sometimes when I am getting ready for bed, Grandma comes over to my sleeping bag and whispers in her night voice, "Abbey, Abbey, wake up and come with me outside. There's something special in the sky."

I get up and we both tiptoe in our nighties and we stand barefoot in the wet grass and the night wind blows. We gaze up at the starry sky and Grandma says, "Look, there's Lyra and Cygnus and Sagittarius and Capricorn." I say, "Speak English!" And she laughs her soft night laugh and says, "There's the Magic Harp, the Swan, the Archer, and the Sea Goat." I look up and try to find the star pictures in the sky.

At the end of the summer Grandma closes up the island cabin. She puts shutters on all the windows and locks the door, and we all go back to the city.

All winter long, even though she wears shoes that make her taller and does city things, I know that she is really my Island Grandma. She swims in dark sea pools and makes cloud stories and flower caves and cookies shaped like moons and stars.

She sails in her boat called *Memory* and she steers and I pull on the ropes at important times.

++ Lasky

My island grandma